CW01220126

The Complete BRICK BIBLE for Kids

The Complete
BRICK BIBLE for Kids

Six Classic Bible Stories

Brendan Powell Smith

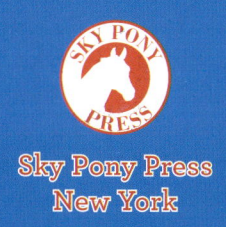

Sky Pony Press
New York

Copyright © 2015 by Brendan Powell Smith

All rights reserved. No part of this book may be reproduced in any manner without the express written consent of the publisher, except in the case of brief excerpts in critical reviews or articles. All inquiries should be addressed to Sky Pony Press, 307 West 36th Street, 11th Floor, New York, NY 10018.

Sky Pony Press books may be purchased in bulk at special discounts for sales promotion, corporate gifts, fund-raising, or educational purposes. Special editions can also be created to specifications. For details, contact the Special Sales Department, Sky Pony Press, 307 West 36th Street, 11th Floor, New York, NY 10018 or info@skyhorsepublishing.com.

Sky Pony® is a registered trademark of Skyhorse Publishing, Inc.®, a Delaware corporation.

Visit our website at www.skyponypress.com.

10 9 8 7 6 5 4 3 2

Manufactured in China, March 2018
This product conforms to CPSIA 2008

Library of Congress Cataloging-in-Publication Data is available on file.

Cover design by Brian Peterson
Cover photo credit Brendan Powell Smith

Print ISBN: 978-1-63450-209-2
Ebook ISBN: 978-1-63450-919-0

Contents

Noah's Ark	9
Joseph and the Colorful Coat	39
David and Goliath	69
Daniel in the Lions' Den	99
Jonah and the Whale	129
The Christmas Story	159

The Complete
BRICK BIBLE for Kids

Noah's Ark

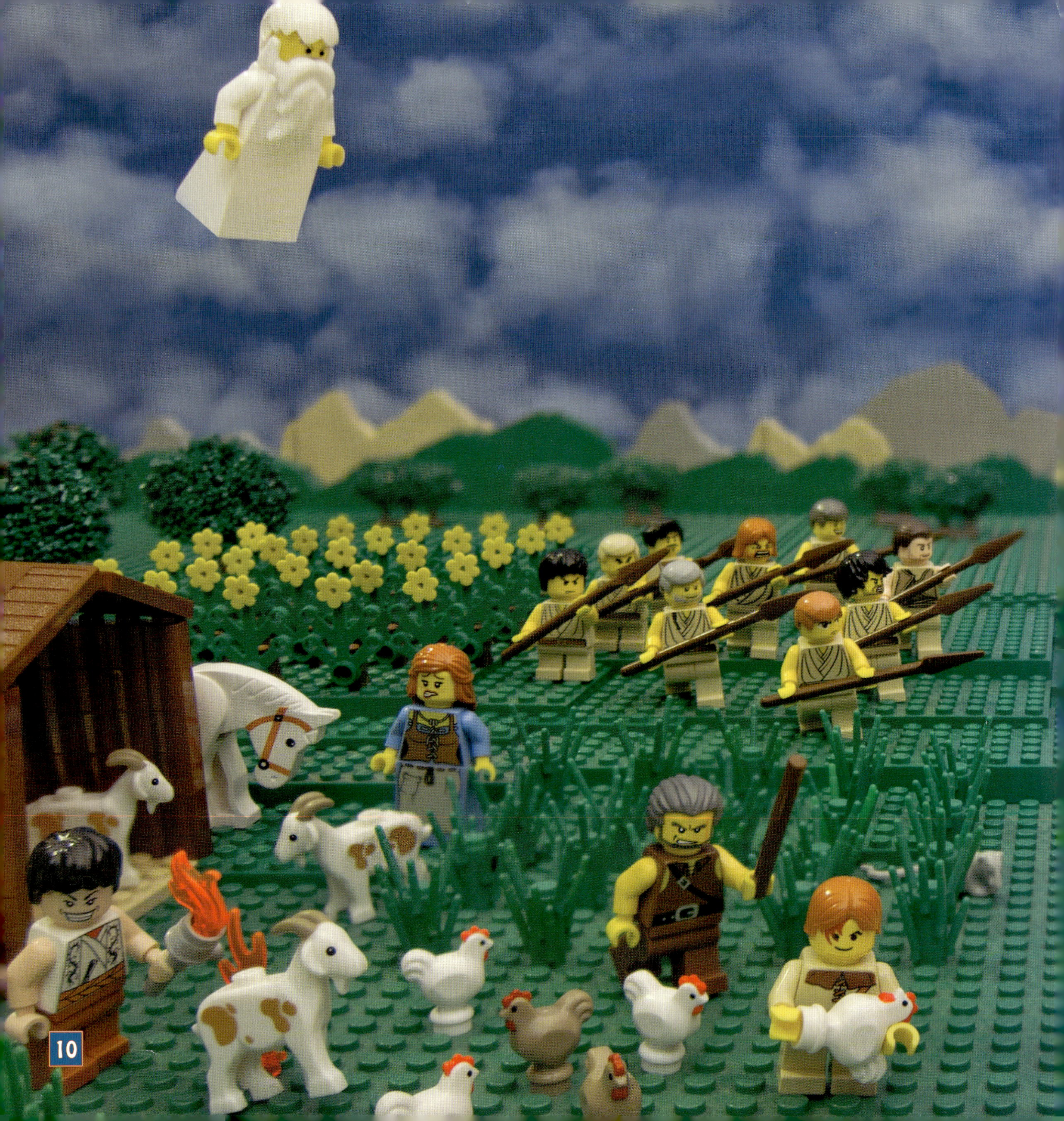

God looked at the world and saw that all the people were very bad.

God decided He would wash away all the people and animals of the world with a giant flood.

Now, in all the world, there was only one good person. His name was Noah. Noah had a wife and three sons.

14

God told Noah to build a big boat called an ark to keep his family safe from the flood.

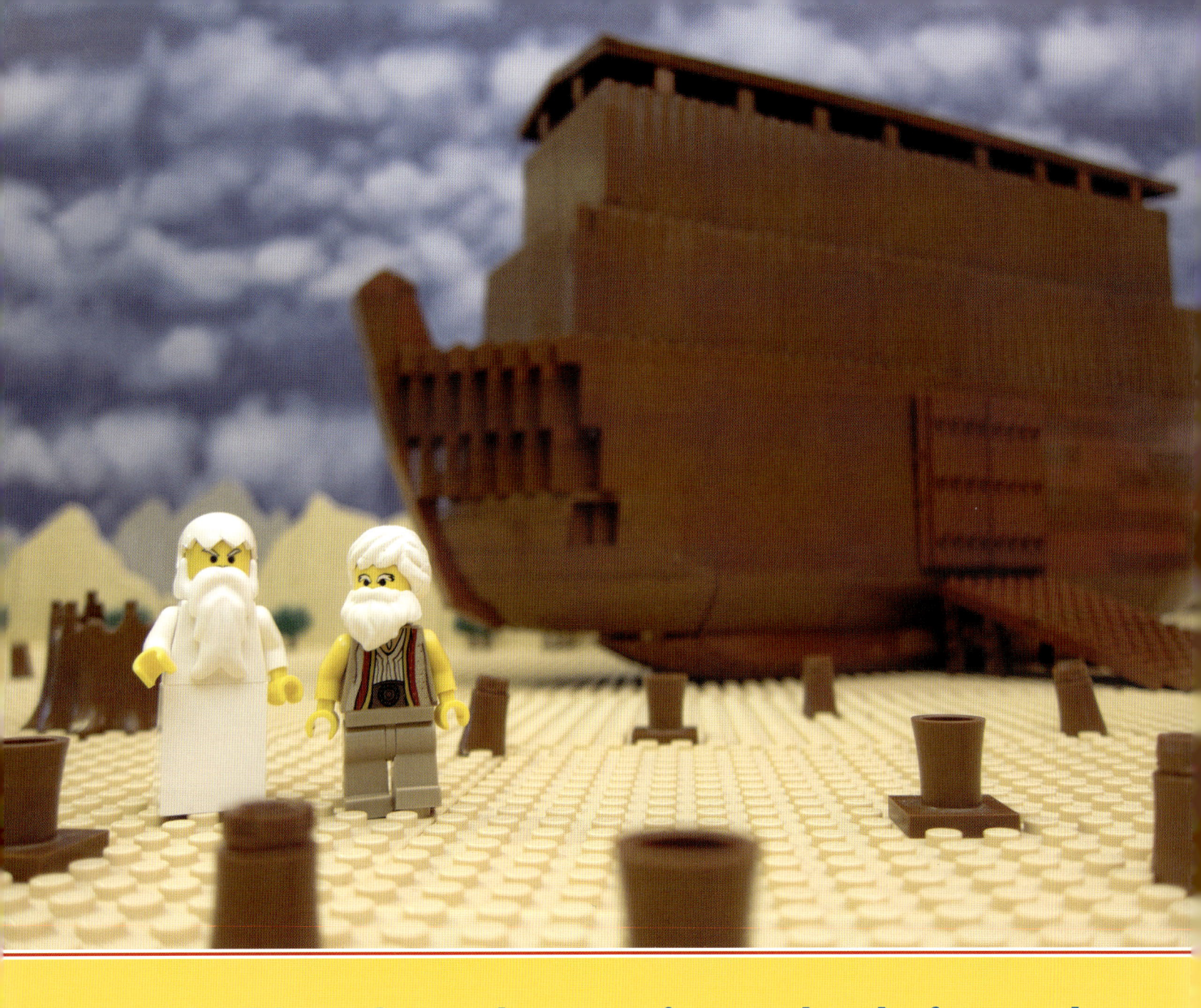

God told Noah to take two of every kind of animal in the world and put them on the ark to keep them safe.

So Noah went out and gathered two of every kind of farm animal.

And two of every kind of wild animal.

18

He gathered two of every type of bird, both big and small.

And two of every living thing that creeps along the ground.

God also told Noah to bring aboard the ark all the kinds of food that all the different animals eat.

22

All the animals entered the ark in pairs.

Finally, God told Noah to bring his family into the ark with him and God shut the doors.

Then God began to flood the world. Water burst up out of the ground and rain poured down from the sky.

25

The water rose so high that the ark Noah built was lifted off the ground.

It rained for forty days and forty nights. The water rose so high that even the tallest mountains were covered, and all the people drowned.

Finally the rain stopped and the ark floated on top of the waters.

29

Months passed and Noah's family stayed inside the ark and fed all the animals.

Then God remembered Noah and lowered the waters. The ark came to rest on top of a mountain.

Noah opened the window of the ark and released a dove. The dove returned to Noah with a branch from an olive tree in its beak.

Then God told Noah it was time for his family and the animals to come out from the ark.

Noah was thankful to God, so he built an altar and made an offering.

God was pleased and promised Noah he would never again drown all the people and animals of the world with a flood.

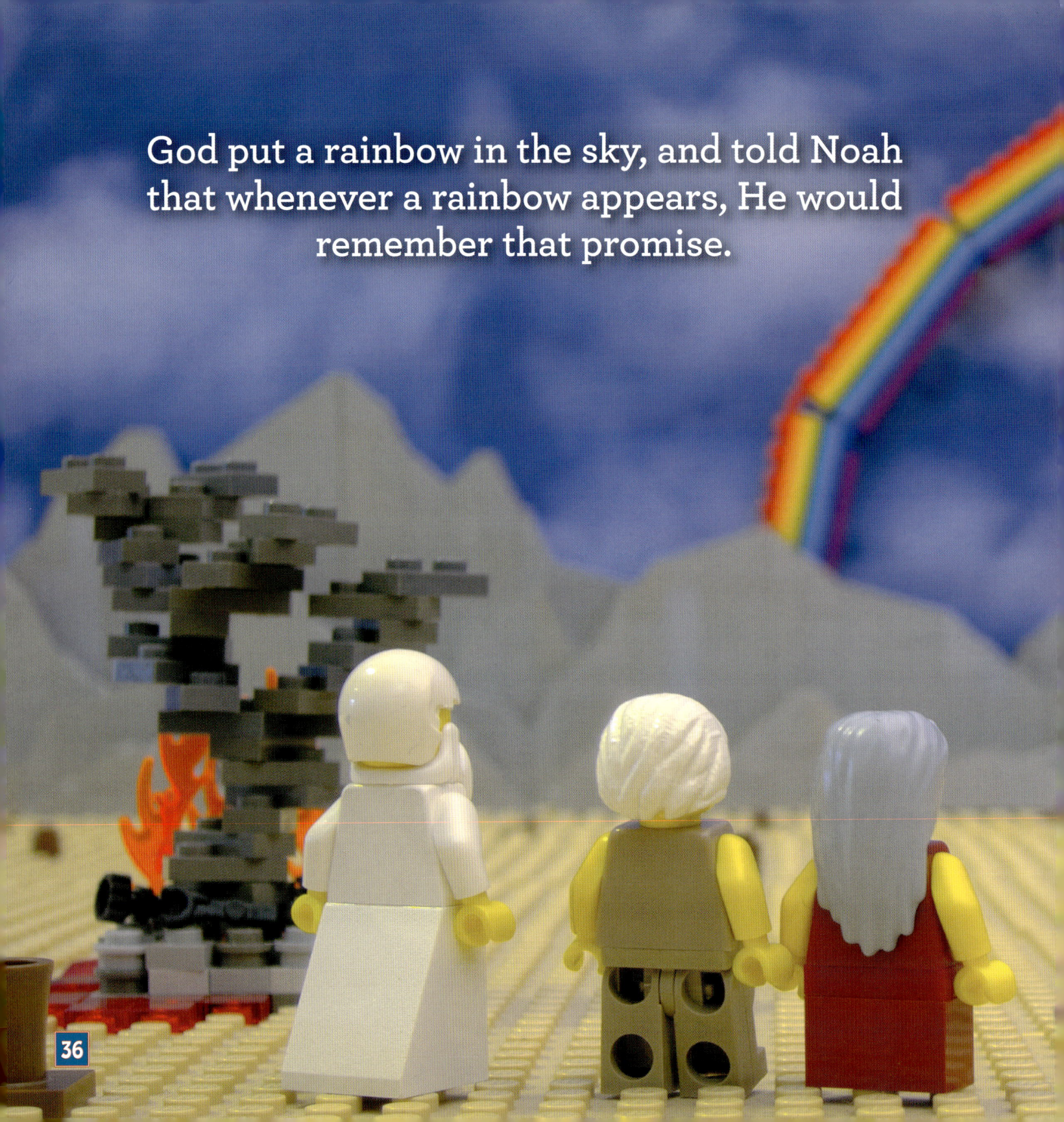

God put a rainbow in the sky, and told Noah that whenever a rainbow appears, He would remember that promise.

37

Activity!

Can you find these ten brick pieces in the story? On which page does each appear? The answers are below.

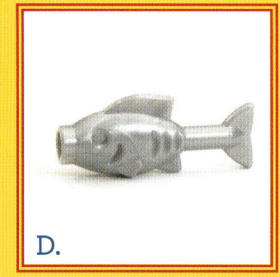

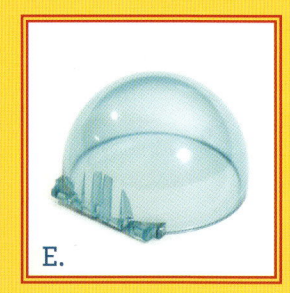

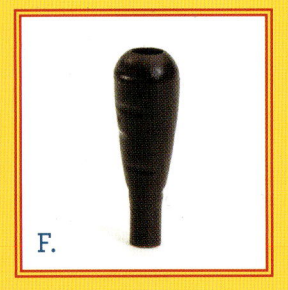

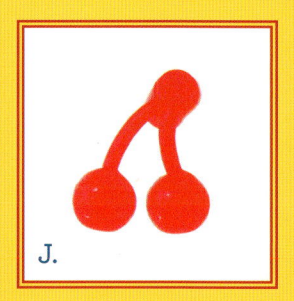

A.

B.

C.

D.

E.

F.

G.

H.

I.

J.

Answer key:

A: pp.14 and 15, B: p.28, C: p.13, D: p.30, E: p.12, F: p.34, G: p.25, H: p.18, I: p.11, J: pp.21 and 30

Joseph and the Colorful Coat

Jacob was an old shepherd with twelve sons. The youngest sons were Joseph and Benjamin. Jacob loved Joseph more than all of his other sons. When Joseph was seventeen years old, his father gave him a special gift—a very colorful coat.

Joseph had strange dreams and told his brothers about them. In his dreams Joseph saw all his brothers bowing down before him. When they heard this, his older brothers got angry and said, "So, you think you are better than us? You think you will rule over us?" Joseph's older brothers hated him.

41

One day, Jacob sent Joseph to check on his older brothers who were watching the family's goats and sheep in the countryside. "Here comes the little dreamer," said his brothers when they saw Joseph approaching, and they quickly made a plan to get rid of him for good.

As soon as Joseph arrived, his brothers grabbed him, tore off his colorful coat, and tossed him into a well that was so deep he couldn't climb out. "Let's see what becomes of his dreams now!" they said.

Shortly afterward, the brothers saw some traveling merchants approaching, and they said, "Let's not leave our brother to die. Let's sell him instead." So they pulled Joseph up out of the well and sold him as a slave to the traveling merchants.

On their way back home, the brothers took Joseph's colorful coat and smeared it with blood from a goat. When they showed it to Jacob, he was deeply heartbroken and said, "My poor son, Joseph! A wild animal must have eaten him!"

Meanwhile, the traveling merchants took Joseph all the way to the land of Egypt. There they sold him to a rich Egyptian man named Potiphar, and Joseph became one of his household slaves.

During his years as a slave, Joseph was successful at every task he performed. Potiphar noticed that Joseph must be blessed by God, so he promoted him to be his personal assistant. Eventually, he put Joseph in charge of his entire household.

Potiphar's wife had noticed that Joseph was very handsome. She would often try to kiss Joseph, but Joseph always turned away. This made her very angry, and one day when Joseph refused to kiss her, she screamed so loud that her husband came running.

When Potiphar arrived, his wife lied to him about Joseph, saying that Joseph had tried to kiss her. Potiphar believed his wife, and he became so angry at Joseph that he had Joseph arrested and thrown in prison.

God still watched over Joseph in prison. When Joseph's fellow prisoners had strange dreams, they would tell him their dreams, and with God's help Joseph always explained exactly what the dream revealed about the future, and he was always right.

One night, Pharaoh, the king of Egypt, had a troubling dream. He very badly wanted to know its meaning, so the next day he gathered all the magicians and wise men in Egypt to his palace and he described his troubling dream to them.

But none of the magicians and wise men could understand Pharaoh's dream or tell him what it meant. Then one of Pharaoh's servants spoke up and said: "I once met a man in prison named Joseph who can explain the meaning of any dream."

So Pharaoh had Joseph taken out of prison and brought before him. "I am told you have the power to explain the meaning of any dream," Pharaoh said. "It is not my power, but God's," replied Joseph. "Tell me your dream."

Pharaoh told Joseph that in his dream there were seven fat, healthy cows that came up out of the Nile River. They were then followed by seven scrawny, sickly cows. The skinny cows ate up the fat cows. And that's when Pharaoh woke up, confused and troubled.

"This is what your dream means," said Joseph. "Egypt will have seven good years of plentiful food followed by seven years of terrible famine when no food will grow. If Pharaoh is wise, he will put someone in charge who will store the extra food from the plentiful years so there is still food to eat during the years of famine."

"Since God has given you such wisdom, there can be no one better suited for the job than you," said Pharaoh to Joseph. "You shall serve as governor over all my lands. I put my entire kingdom in your power, and my people shall obey your commands."

As Joseph predicted, Egypt then had seven years of plenty during which more grain was grown than all the Egyptians could eat. As governor, Joseph made sure all the extra food was safely locked away in Pharaoh's great storehouses.

Then the years of terrible famine arrived, and no food was able to grow anywhere. The only food around was in Egypt thanks to Joseph's careful planning. Starving people from all the surrounding lands traveled to Egypt to buy food from Joseph.

In Joseph's homeland of Israel, the famine was severe, and the elderly Jacob said to his eleven remaining sons, "Why are you all just standing around here while we starve? Travel to Egypt where they have food and bring some back home!"

So the brothers set out, and when they reached Egypt, they bowed down before the governor and humbly asked for food. They did not recognize that the governor was their own brother Joseph. But Joseph recognized his brothers.

Joseph wondered if his brothers had changed their ways after all these years, so he decided to test them. He had their sacks filled with grain, but he also hid some money in their sacks. And in his younger brother Benjamin's sack, he hid his own silver drinking cup.

61

Joseph sent them on their way home, but soon afterward he chased them down as they were leaving the city. "Why have you stolen from me after I was kind and gave you food?" shouted Joseph. He had their sacks opened to reveal the money and the silver cup.

The brothers were shocked and confused. They said to themselves that God must now be punishing them for the awful thing they did to their brother so many years ago. "Because your youngest brother stole my cup," said Joseph, "I will keep him as my slave."

At this the oldest brother begged Joseph to take him as a slave instead of Benjamin. He told Joseph that their father had already lost one of his sons, and to now lose the youngest son would break his heart forever.

Joseph now saw that his brothers had indeed changed their ways and he could pretend no longer. "Look closely! Don't you recognize me? I am your brother Joseph," he told them. "Now, go return to our father and bring him and all of our family here to Egypt."

Jacob was amazed and overjoyed to learn that his son Joseph was still alive. He took his entire family and traveled down to Egypt. When they finally met again after so many years, Joseph and Jacob hugged and wept tears of joy.

Pharaoh was grateful to Joseph and he gave Joseph's family the best land in Egypt for their new home. Joseph was not angry with his brothers for what they did to him when he was young, because he knew it had all been part of God's plan.

67

Activity!

Can you find these ten brick pieces in the story? On which page does each appear? The answers are below.

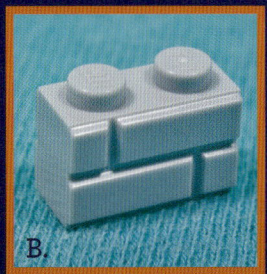

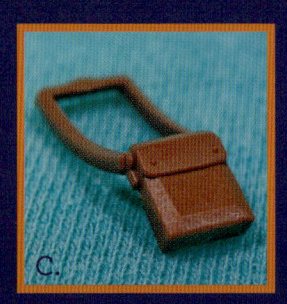

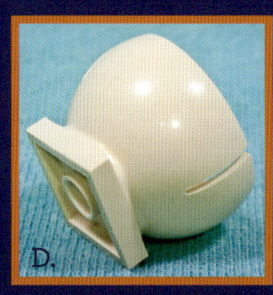

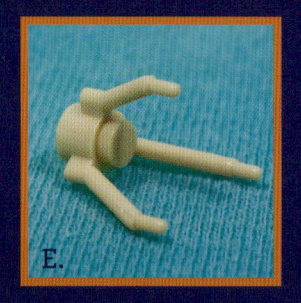

A.

B.

C.

D.

E.

F.

G.

H.

I.

J.

Answer key:

A: p.59, B: p.43, C: p.44, D: p.49, E: p.57, F: p.51, G: p.67, H: p.66, I: p.47, J: p.52

68

David and Goliath

God's people, the Israelites, were at war with the Philistines.

The army of each nation stood facing each other, ready for battle.

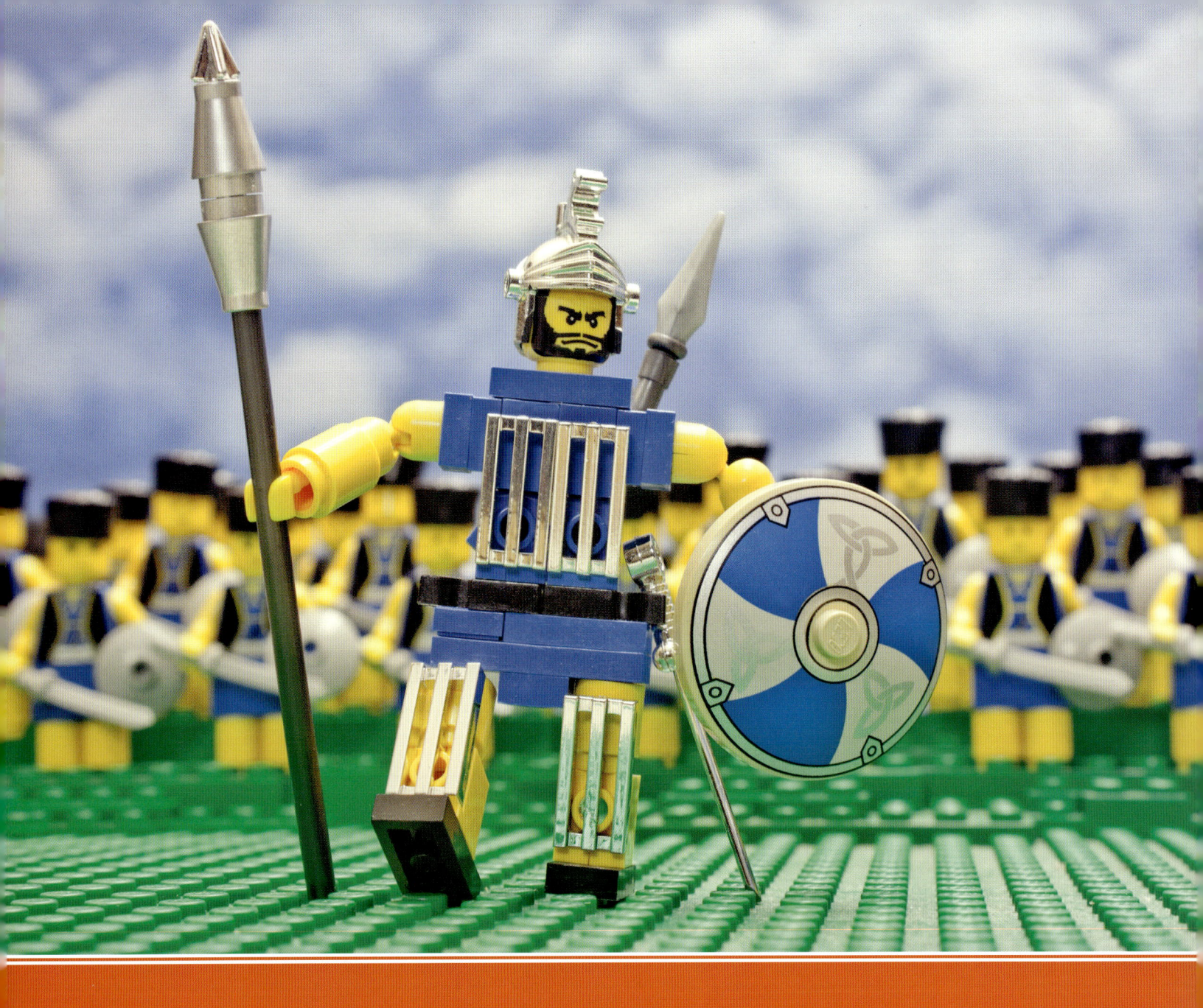

Among the Philistines was a giant named Goliath.
He carried a huge spear and shield
and wore a bronze helmet and armor.

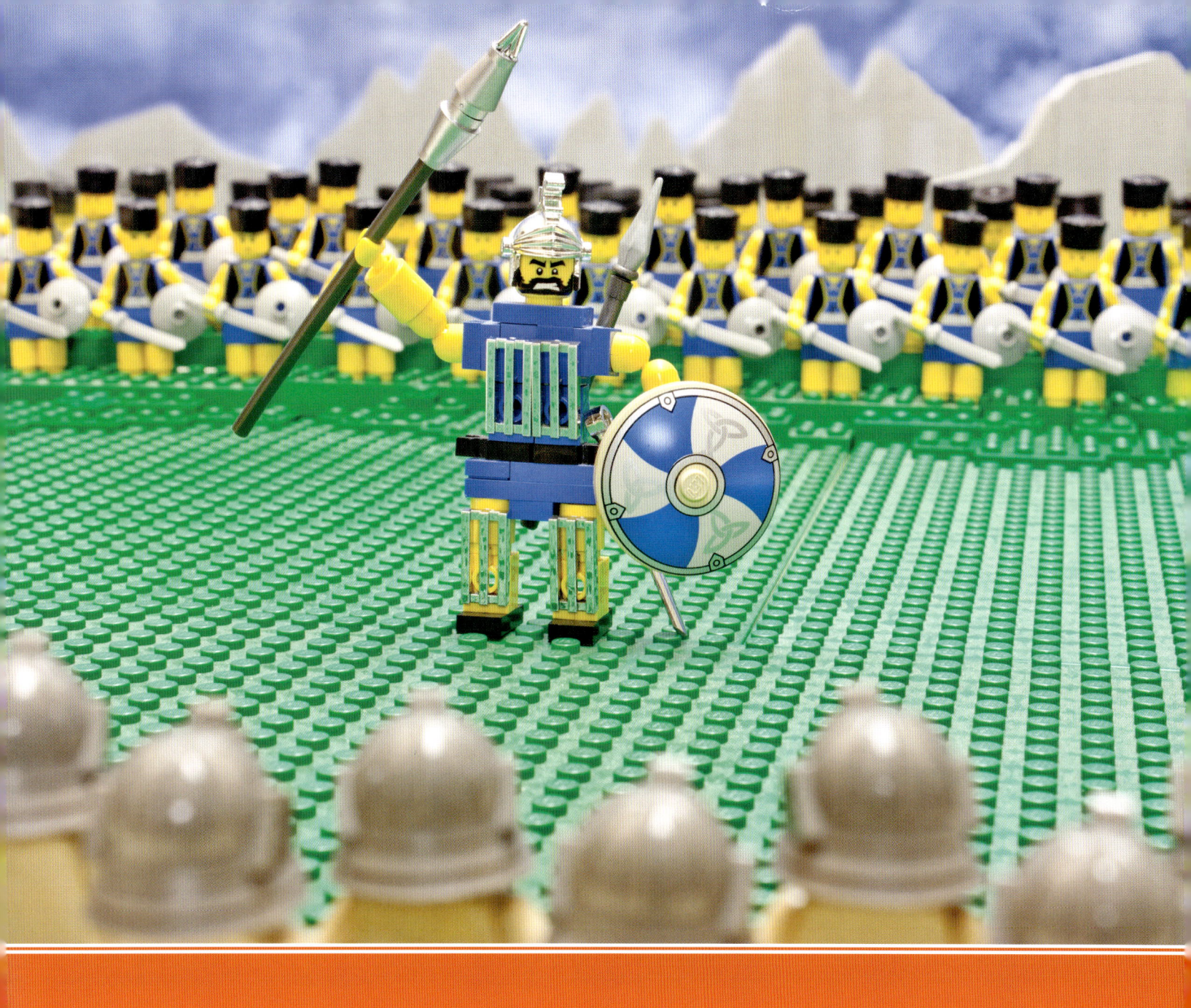

Goliath made a challenge to the Israelites, saying, "Send one of your men out to fight me. If he defeats me, we will be become your slaves. If I defeat him, you will become our slaves."

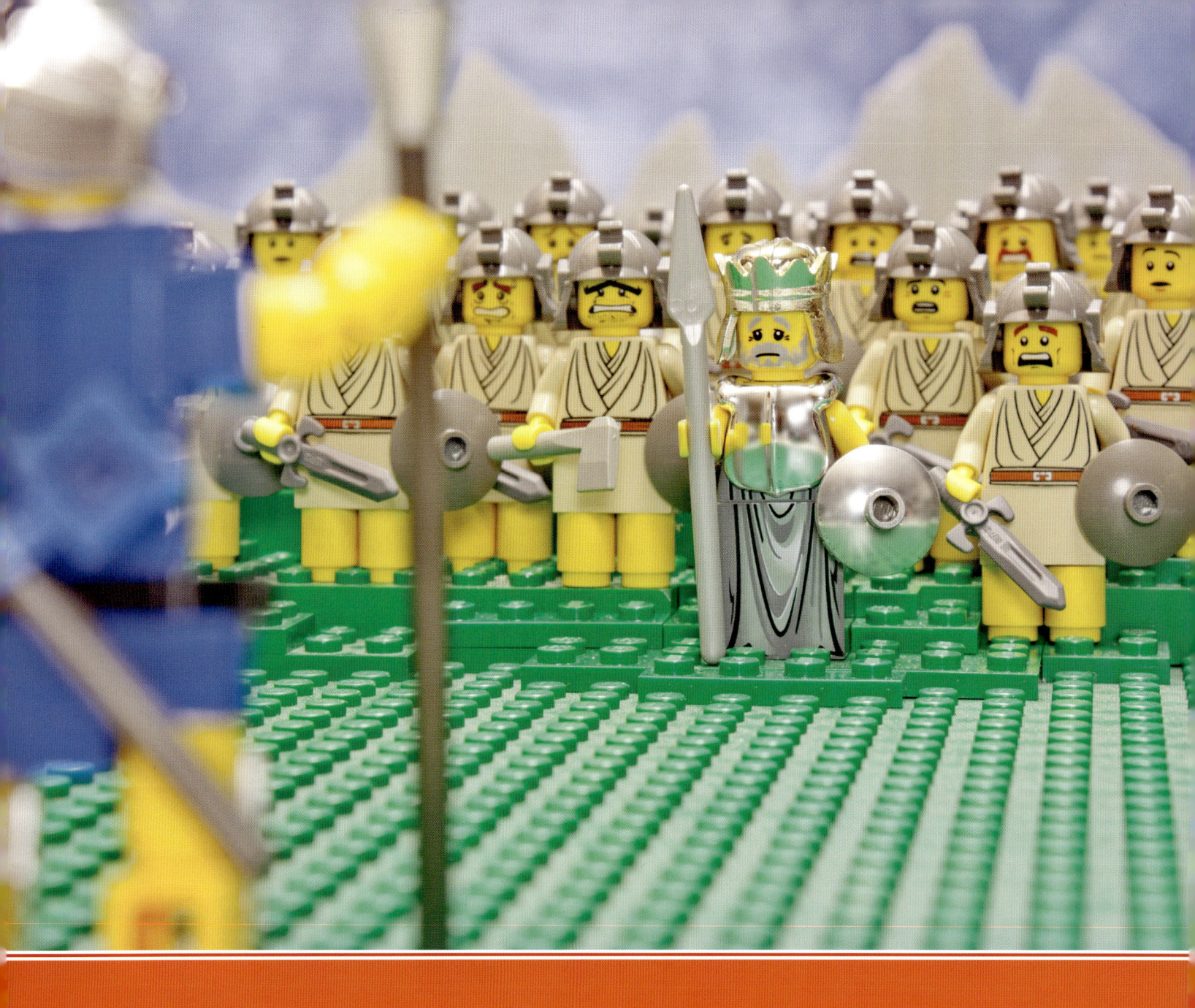

When they heard this, King Saul and the Israelites were terrified!

Miles away, in the town of Bethlehem, an Israelite boy named David was busy watching over his father's sheep, keeping them safe.

If a lion or a bear tried to eat one of the sheep, David would chase after it.

He would grab it by the neck and strike it dead.

That day, however, David's father said to him, "Take this bread and this cheese to your older brothers in the army. See how they are doing and return to me with news."

So David traveled to where the army was preparing for battle. He left the bread and cheese with the supply keeper and ran to the front lines to find his brothers.

Just then, Goliath again stepped forward to challenge the Israelites, saying, "Send one of your men out to fight me." And David heard this.

David asked the men standing near him, "What reward will be given to the man who kills this Philistine?" And they told him, "The King will give him great riches, and he will get to marry the princess."

David went to King Saul and said, "I will go out and fight this Philistine." But King Saul told him, "You are just a boy, and the giant has been a warrior all his life! You can't fight him!"

David told King Saul, "God protected me when I killed lions and bears, and God will protect me when I kill this giant who has challenged God's army."

King Saul said to David, "Go then, and may God be with you!" He gave David his royal armor and his sword and shield. But David said, "I can't walk like this! I'm not used to these things."

David took off all the armor and went to a stream to gather some smooth stones. He put them in his pockets.

86

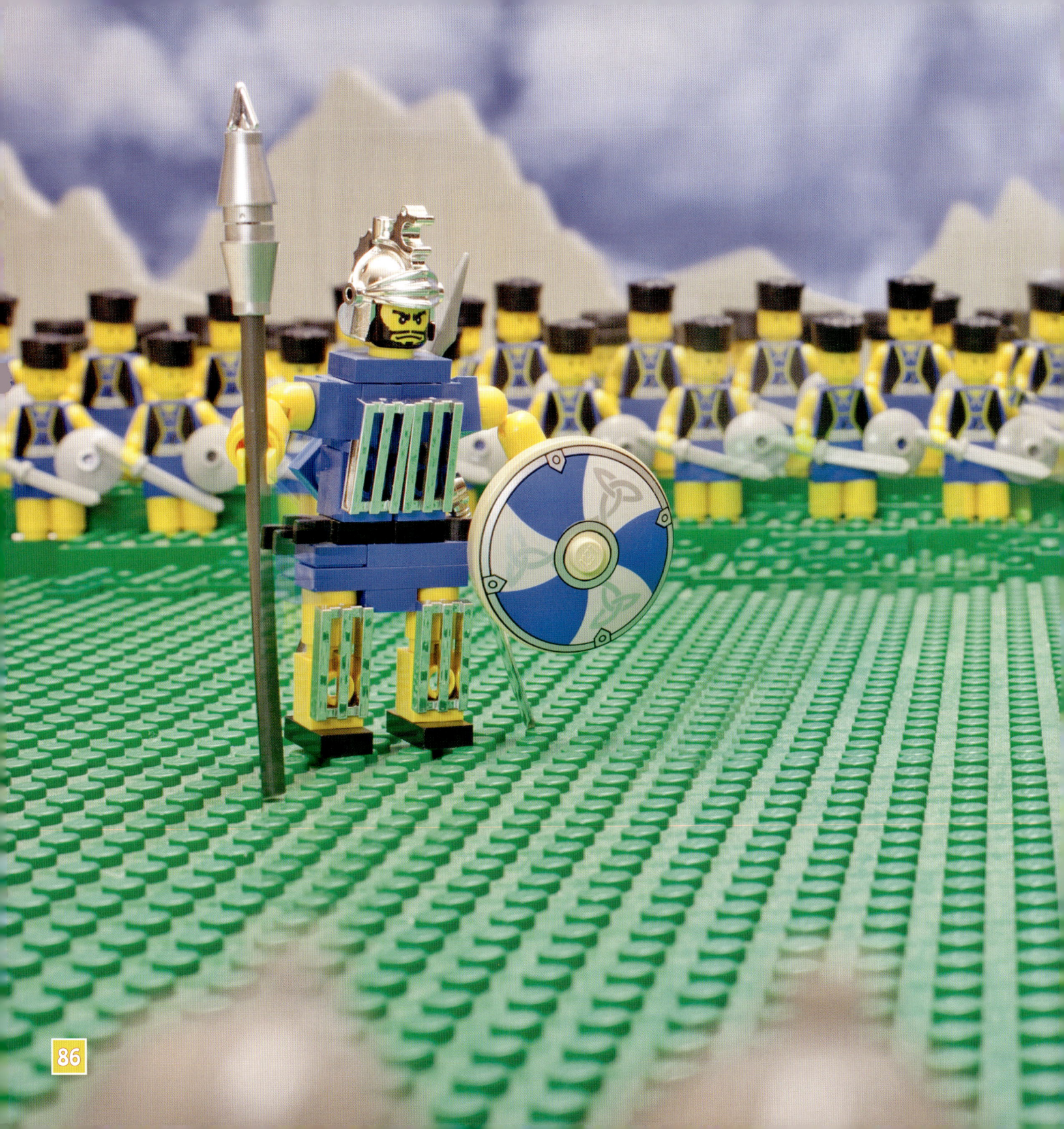

Carrying only his walking stick and a sling, David went out to face Goliath the giant.

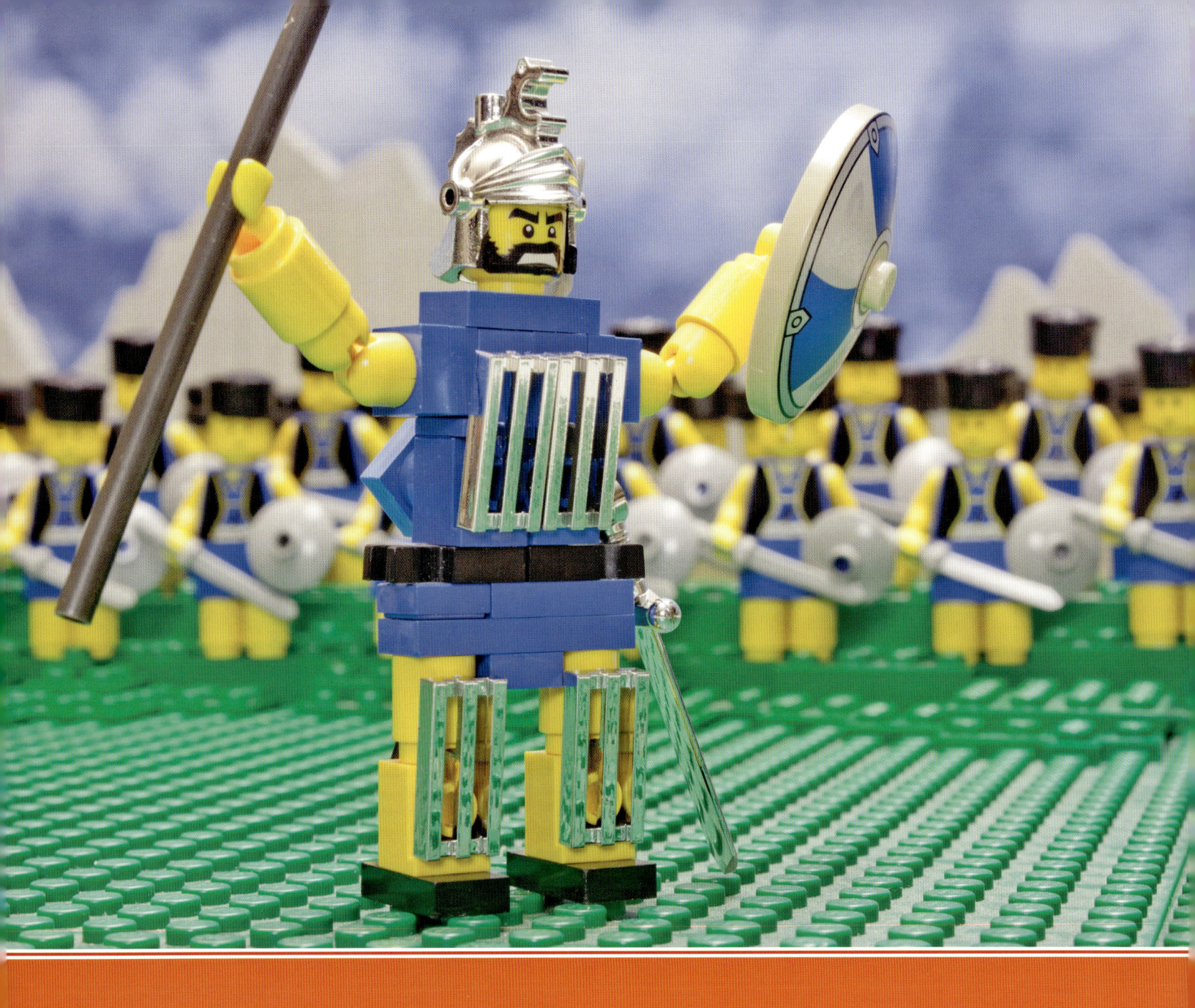

Goliath was insulted to see that such a small boy had come out to fight him. He said to David, "Do you think I am merely a dog? Is this why you come at me with a stick?"

But David said to him, "I have God on my side, and you have chosen to fight God's army. Today I will kill you and cut off your head."

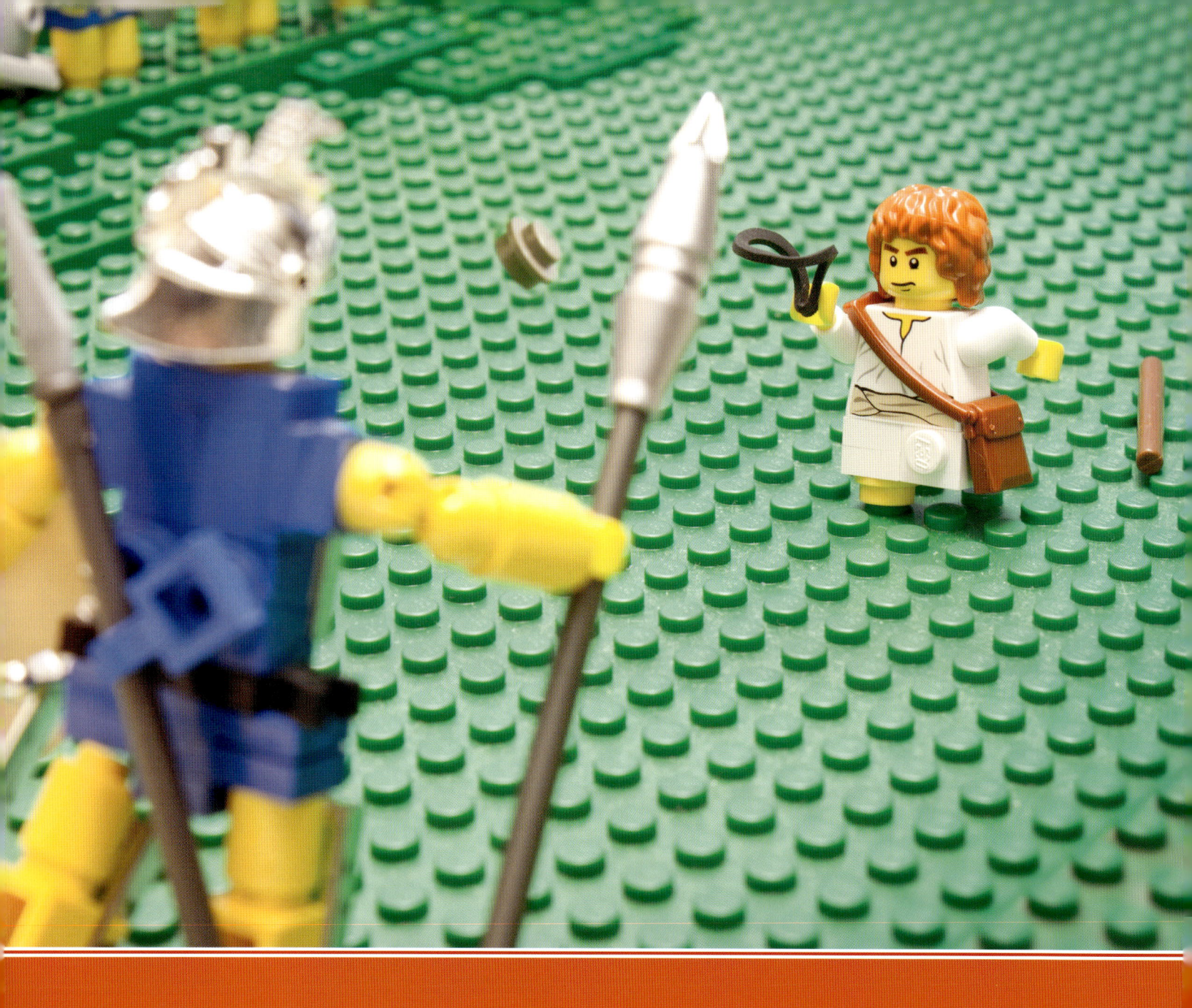

Goliath got angry and moved closer to attack. David took a stone from his pocket and used his sling to launch it at the giant.

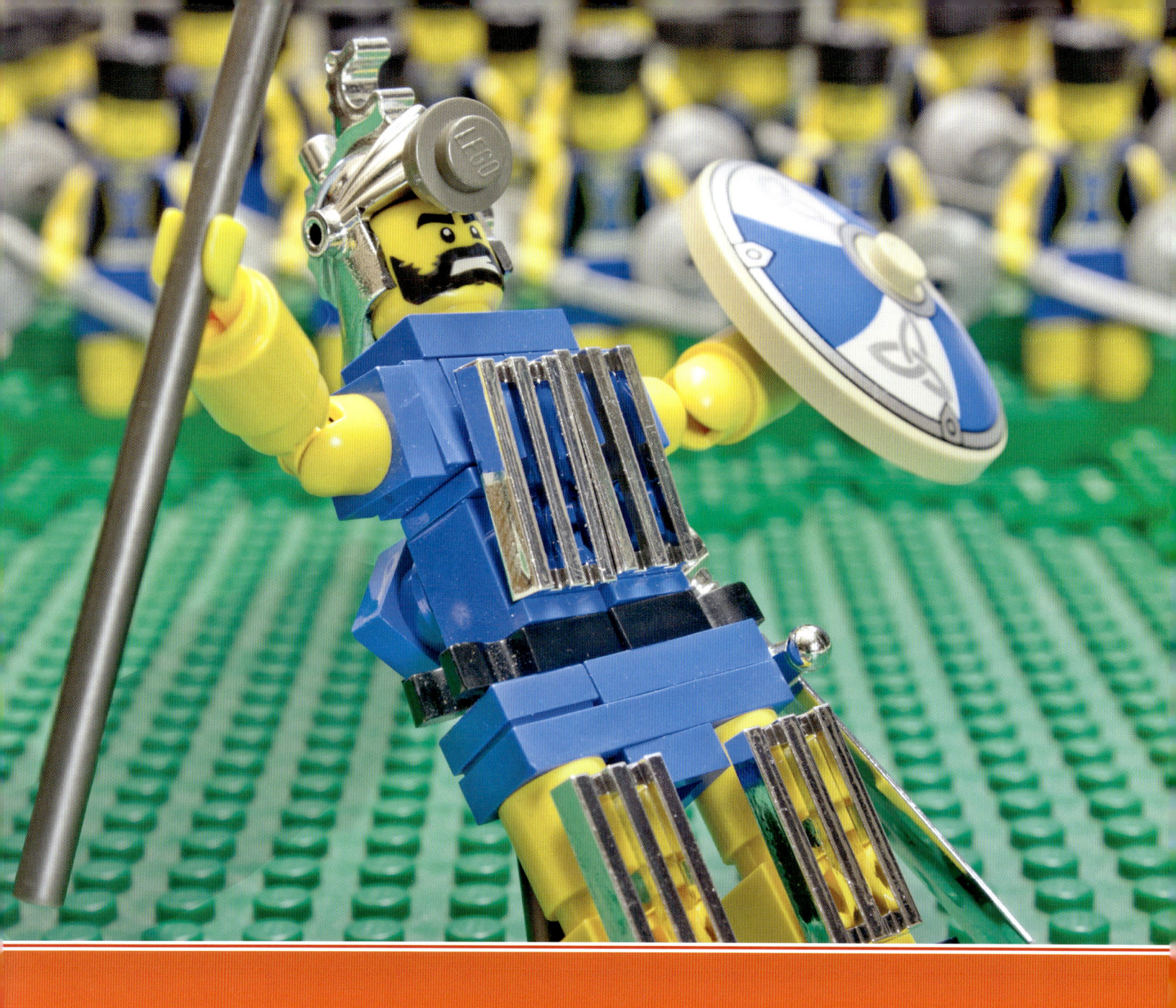

The stone hit Goliath in the forehead.

Goliath fell down dead. David took the giant's sword and cut off his head.

When the Philistines saw that their champion was dead, they ran away in fear.

The Israelites chased after them and killed many of the Philistines that day. Then the Israelites collected the food and the weapons left behind by the Philistines.

David took the head of Goliath to Jerusalem. The people of Israel treated him as a hero and sang songs to praise him.

When David grew up, he married King Saul's daughter, the princess Michal.

And God chose David to be the next King of Israel.

Activity!

Can you find these ten brick pieces in the story? On which page does each appear? The answers are below.

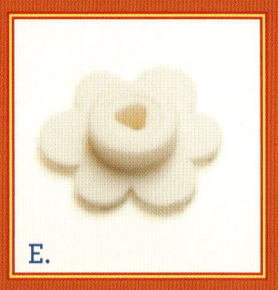

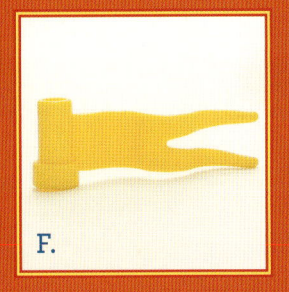

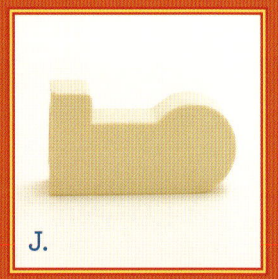

A.	B.	C.	D.	E.
F.	G.	H.	I.	J.

Answer key:

A: p.74, B: p.95, C: p.79, D: p.96, E: pp.94 and 96, F: p.82, G: p.85, H: p.83, I: p.78, J: p.78

Daniel in the Lions' Den

King Nebuchadnezzar and his army conquered Israel where God's people, the Israelites, lived. Then he took all the Israelites with him back to the city of Babylon where his people had a different religion. One of the Israelites who was taken to Babylon was a young boy named Daniel.

Daniel and his three friends from Israel were smart, good looking boys. The king put them in a special school so they would grow up to be very wise and would help the king rule over his enormous kingdom. With God's help, Daniel and his friends became very wise indeed.

One day the king had his people build a giant golden statue. The king ordered everyone to worship the statue, and he said that anyone who did not worship the giant statue would be thrown into a blazing furnace of fire.

Some of the Babylonians noticed that Daniel's three friends only worshipped God and did not worship the golden statue.

When the king found out, he became very angry. He had Daniel's three friends tied up and ordered two of his strongest soldiers to lift up the three friends and toss them into the blazing furnace.

The fire in the furnace was so hot that flames were leaping out. As Daniel's three friends were tossed into the furnace, the two soldiers caught on fire and were burned up.

Daniel's friends stood inside the blazing furnace, but they were not harmed. As the king looked on, he noticed a fourth figure had joined them amid the flames. He saw that it was an angel sent by God to protect Daniel's three friends.

The king ordered the three friends to come out of the fire, and he was amazed to see they had not been harmed. The king gained respect for their God and he made this announcement to his people: "Anyone who says anything bad about the God of the Israelites will be put to death."

One day, the king woke up from a frightening dream. In the dream he saw a very tall tree. There were birds living in the tree, and there were wild animals living below the tree in its shade. Then an angel appeared and announced that the tree would be cut down.

The king gathered his wise men and told them the dream, but no one could tell him what it meant. Finally, the king told the dream to Daniel. Daniel knew what the dream meant, but was afraid to tell the king. The king insisted.

So Daniel told the king its meaning. "You have grown very big and strong, like the tree in your dream," said Daniel. "But God has decided that you will be humbled for a time and live among the wild animals."

And so it happened one day that the king was walking along the roof of his royal palace, admiring the view of the city. "Here is the great city of Babylon," he said, "which has been built by my mighty strength for my honor and glory."

At that very moment, the king suddenly found himself among the wild animals, far away from any cities or towns. He lived like an animal for some time, eating grass and sleeping outdoors. His hair grew long, and his fingernails grew into claws.

After some time passed, God returned him to his place as king of Babylon and made him more powerful than before. The king had learned to be humble before the God of Israel. He praised God and marveled at God's power over all humans.

Many years later the king's son became the new king of Babylon. At a great feast for his friends, the new king served wine in golden cups that had been taken from the Temple of the God of the Israelites. During the meal, the Babylonians gave praise to the gods of their religion.

Suddenly the king saw a human hand appear out of nowhere and it began writing something on the wall nearby. The king turned white with fear, and his guests were scared and confused. When the writing was complete, the hand vanished.

The new king gathered all his wise men to read the writing on the wall, but none of them could figure out what it said or what it meant.

Then the queen remembered that many years ago, Daniel had once helped the king's father by telling him what his frightening dream had meant. So Daniel was found and brought to the new king to help him.

117

Daniel could read the writing on the wall and he knew its meaning. He said to the king, "The message says that you have failed to respect the God of Israel and that God will now bring an end to your rule." That very night, the new king was killed.

The next king was named Darius. He chose several assistants to help him rule over his kingdom. Since Daniel was most skilled, the king put him in charge of all his assistants. This made the other assistants jealous of Daniel, and they made a plan to get rid of him.

To get Daniel in trouble, the other assistants convinced King Darius to make a new law. It said that for the next thirty days, if anyone worships anyone other than the king of Babylon, they will be thrown into a den of lions.

Daniel knew about the new law, but continued to worship the God of Israel. So the king's assistants came to Daniel's house and saw him worshipping his God. They told the king about this and reminded him that Daniel must be thrown into a den of lions.

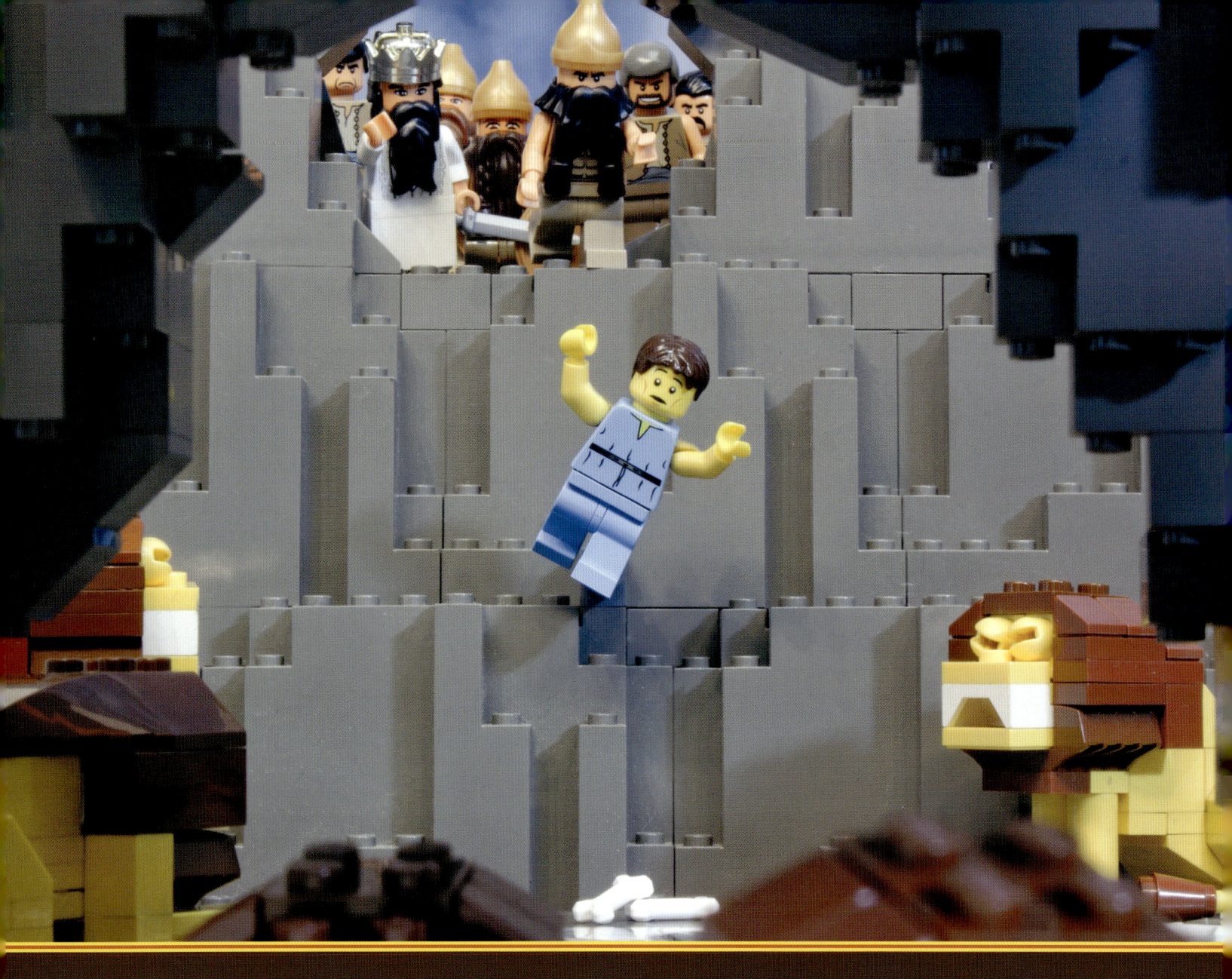

King Darius liked Daniel and did not want to hurt him, but he knew he must do what the new law required. So the king had Daniel thrown into a den of lions, and said to him, "Maybe the God that you always worship will save you from the lions!"

A large stone was rolled over the opening of the lions' den so Daniel could not escape. That night King Darius was so worried about Daniel that he could not eat any food and did not get any sleep.

124

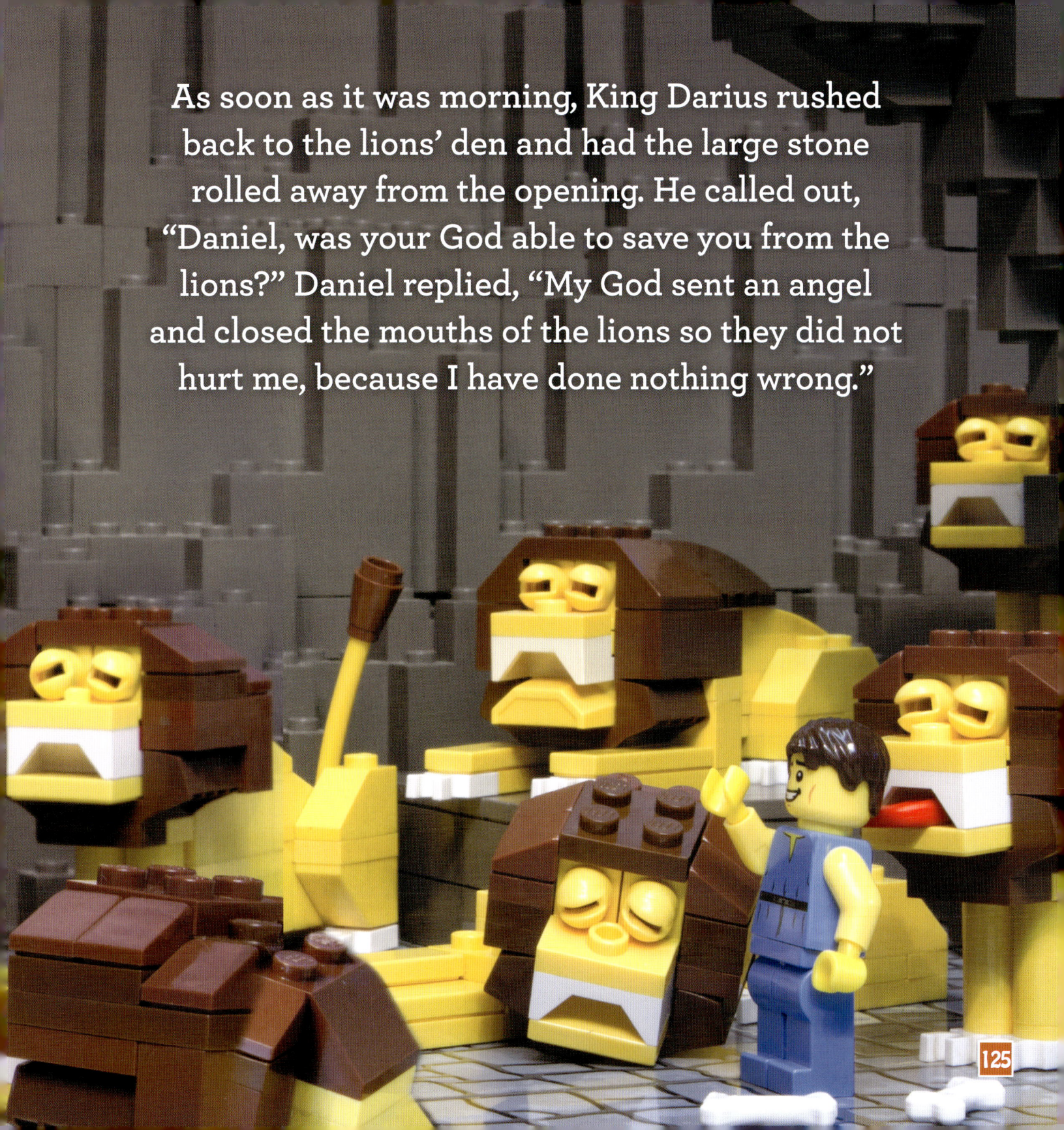

As soon as it was morning, King Darius rushed back to the lions' den and had the large stone rolled away from the opening. He called out, "Daniel, was your God able to save you from the lions?" Daniel replied, "My God sent an angel and closed the mouths of the lions so they did not hurt me, because I have done nothing wrong."

King Darius was amazed. He had Daniel taken up out of the lions' den. Then he ordered the assistants who tried to get rid of Daniel to be thrown into the lions' den with their wives and children. The lions tore them all apart before they even reached the ground.

The king then announced that all the people in the world should shake with fear before the God of the Israelites who rules over the world forever and who saved Daniel from the jaws of the lions.

Activity!

Can you find these ten brick pieces in the story? On which page does each appear? The answers are below.

A.
B.
C.
D.
E.
F.
G.
H.
I.
J.

Answer key:

A: p.121, B: p.103, C: p.127, D: p.111, E: p.116, F: p.102, G: p.120, H: p.101, I: p.108, J: p.109

Jonah and the Whale

One day God said to Jonah, "The people in the faraway city of Nineveh have been very bad. I want you to go there and tell the people that I know how bad they have been, and that I will soon punish them severely!"

But Jonah did not want to do this. Instead, he ran away from God.

131

He found some sailors who were taking their ship in the opposite direction from Nineveh and went with them.

While the ship was at sea, God sent a powerful storm against them.

The sailors were terrified that their ship would break apart in the roaring wind and mighty waves.

The sailors cried out to the heavens for help. As water began to fill the ship, they had to throw all their cargo overboard to keep it from sinking.

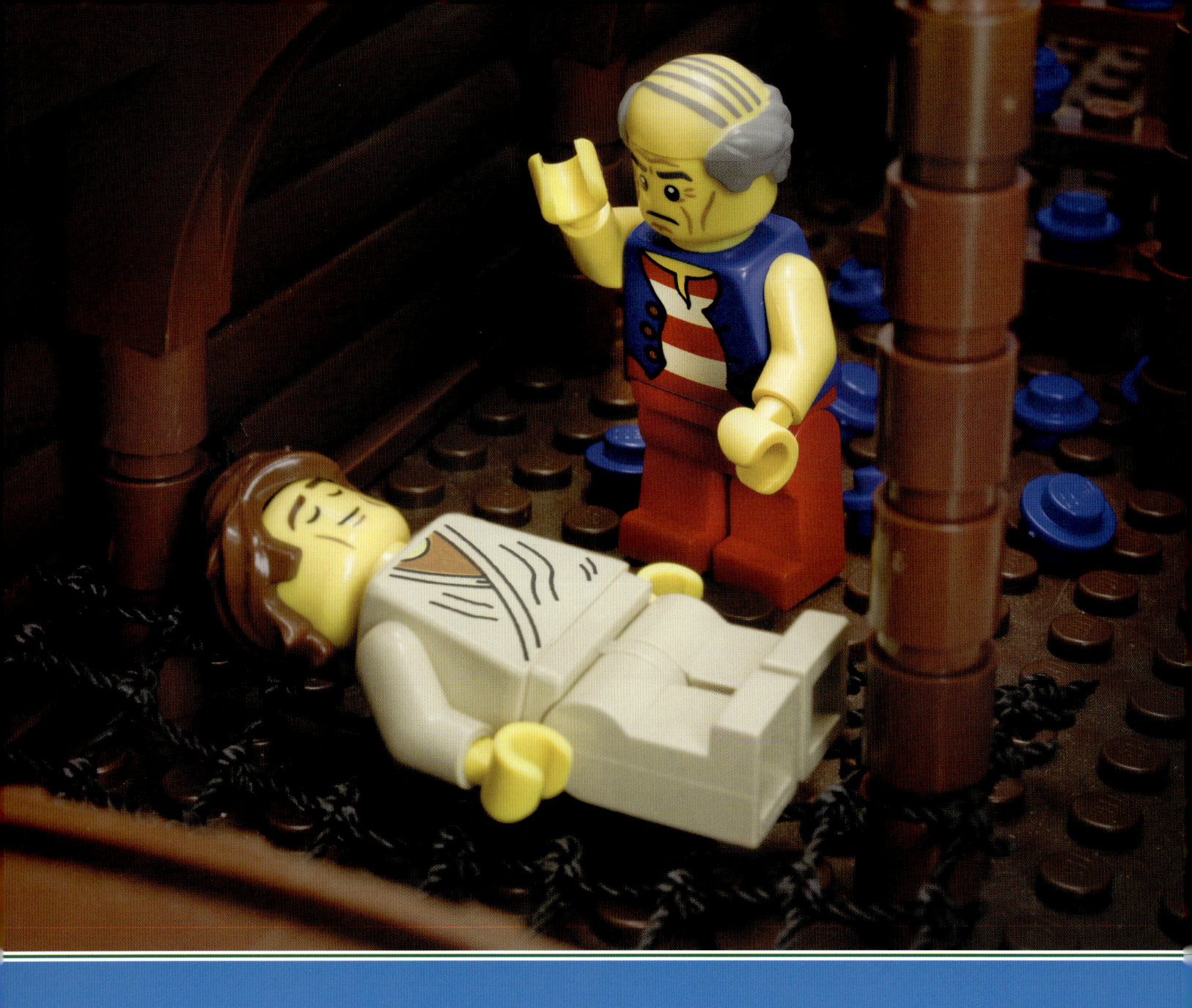

Meanwhile, below deck, Jonah was sound asleep. The captain of the ship came to him and said, "How can you sleep at a time like this? Wake up and ask your God to save us from this storm!"

Jonah got up and told the sailors, "Listen! It is my fault that we are all in danger. I tried to run away from God. The only way to end the storm is to throw me overboard!"

The sailors did not want Jonah to drown in the raging sea, but the storm was growing worse by the minute. So they asked God to forgive them, and they lifted up Jonah and tossed him over the edge of the ship.

As soon as Jonah was in the water, the sea calmed and the storm ended. The sailors celebrated and praised God.

140

Then God sent a huge whale that swallowed Jonah.

Jonah was in the belly of the whale for three days and nights. While there, he prayed to God to rescue him and promised to worship Him in the future.

142

Then God commanded the whale to spit Jonah out onto dry land.

Again God said to Jonah, "Go to the faraway city of Nineveh and tell them that I know how bad they have been, and that I will soon punish them severely!"

This time Jonah immediately set off for Nineveh. After many days, he arrived at the great capital of the Assyrian Empire, a city that was home to over 120,000 people.

Nineveh was a huge city that took three days to walk across. Once Jonah had walked for a full day, he began to announce, "In forty days, God will completely destroy this city!"

When Nineveh's king heard this, he said that everyone must stop being bad and stop hurting others. He ordered the people and animals to stop eating and drinking so God would see they were serious about changing their ways.

Everyone in Nineveh did just what the king ordered. They stopped being bad and hurting other people. And they did not let anyone or any animals eat or drink anything.

Jonah left the city and walked a distance away. He then sat down in the hot sun to watch God destroy the city.

When God saw that the people of Nineveh were serious about changing their ways, however, He decided not to destroy them and their city as He had said He would do. This made Jonah very angry.

He said to God, "I knew that if the people of Nineveh changed their ways, you would forgive them because you are merciful! I ran away from you and did not warn them because I wanted you to give them the punishment they deserved!"

151

But God said to Jonah, "Is it right for you to be so angry?"

As Jonah continued to watch the city, God caused the little plant next to Jonah to grow tall and provide him with shade. Jonah was happy to have this plant bring him relief from the terrible heat of the sun.

The next morning, however, God caused the plant to dry up and die. And all day the sun beat down on Jonah, and he became very angry that his plant had died.

Then God said to Jonah, "Are you really so concerned about this little plant?" And Jonah replied, "Yes! I am very angry about it!"

155

God said, "If you have such concern over a little plant, shouldn't I show even more concern for a huge city full of people and animals?"

Jonah began his long walk home having learned something about how God treats His creations.

Activity!

Can you find these ten brick pieces in the story? On which page does each appear? The answers are below.

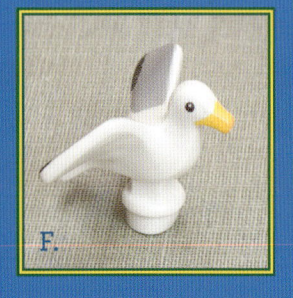

A.
B.
C.
D.
E.
F.
G.
H.
I.
J.

Answer key:

A: p.147, B: p.140, C: p.153, D: p.132, E: p.144, F: p.143, G: p.146, H: p.130, I: p.163, J: p.148

The Christmas Story

This is the story of how Jesus Christ was born.

In the town of Nazareth, a young woman named Mary was engaged to a man named Joseph, but they were not yet married.

161

One day God sent the angel Gabriel to tell Mary, "You will soon give birth to a boy named Jesus, and he will be called the Son of God."

Mary was very surprised and asked, "How can this be? I am not even married." The angel replied, "Nothing is impossible for God."

When Joseph found out Mary was pregnant, he decided to call off their engagement and send Mary away.

But an angel appeared to Joseph in a dream and said, "The child inside Mary was put there by the Holy Spirit. Do not be afraid to marry her."

Now at this time, emperor Caesar Augustus ordered everyone in the empire to register for taxes in the town where they were born.

Since Joseph's family was from Bethlehem, he and Mary set out from Nazareth and traveled for a week to reach Joseph's hometown.

While they were in Bethlehem, the time came for the baby to be born. Mary wrapped the newborn child in swaddling clothes.

There was no room at the inn, so she laid the child in a manger.

In a field nearby, shepherds were watching over their flocks at night when an angel appeared and said, "I have good and joyful news! Today a savior has been born, the messiah! You will find him wrapped in swaddling clothes, lying in a manger."

171

So the shepherds hurried away and found Mary and Joseph and the baby lying in the manger. The shepherds repeated what the angel had told them about the child.

At this time, some magi from the east arrived in Jerusalem and asked, "Where is the newborn King of the Jews? We saw his star in the sky and have come to worship him."

King Herod heard about this and he was very worried. Everyone in the city of Jerusalem was very worried.

He summoned the magi and told them, "Go and find this child. Then return to me, so that I may also go and worship him."

The magi saw the star again, and they followed it until it stood still over the place where the child was.

177

Entering the house, the magi saw the child with his mother Mary. They knelt to worship him and presented him with gifts of gold, frankincense, and myrrh.

In a dream, the magi were warned not to return to King Herod. So they set out to return to their own country by a different route.

Then an angel appeared to Joseph in a dream and warned him, "Flee to Egypt, for King Herod is searching for the child so he can kill him!"

So Joseph took the child and his mother and fled to Egypt.

When King Herod realized that he had been tricked by the magi, he was furious.

So he summoned his soldiers and gave them orders.

King Herod told the soldiers to kill all the children under the age of two in Bethlehem and the surrounding region.

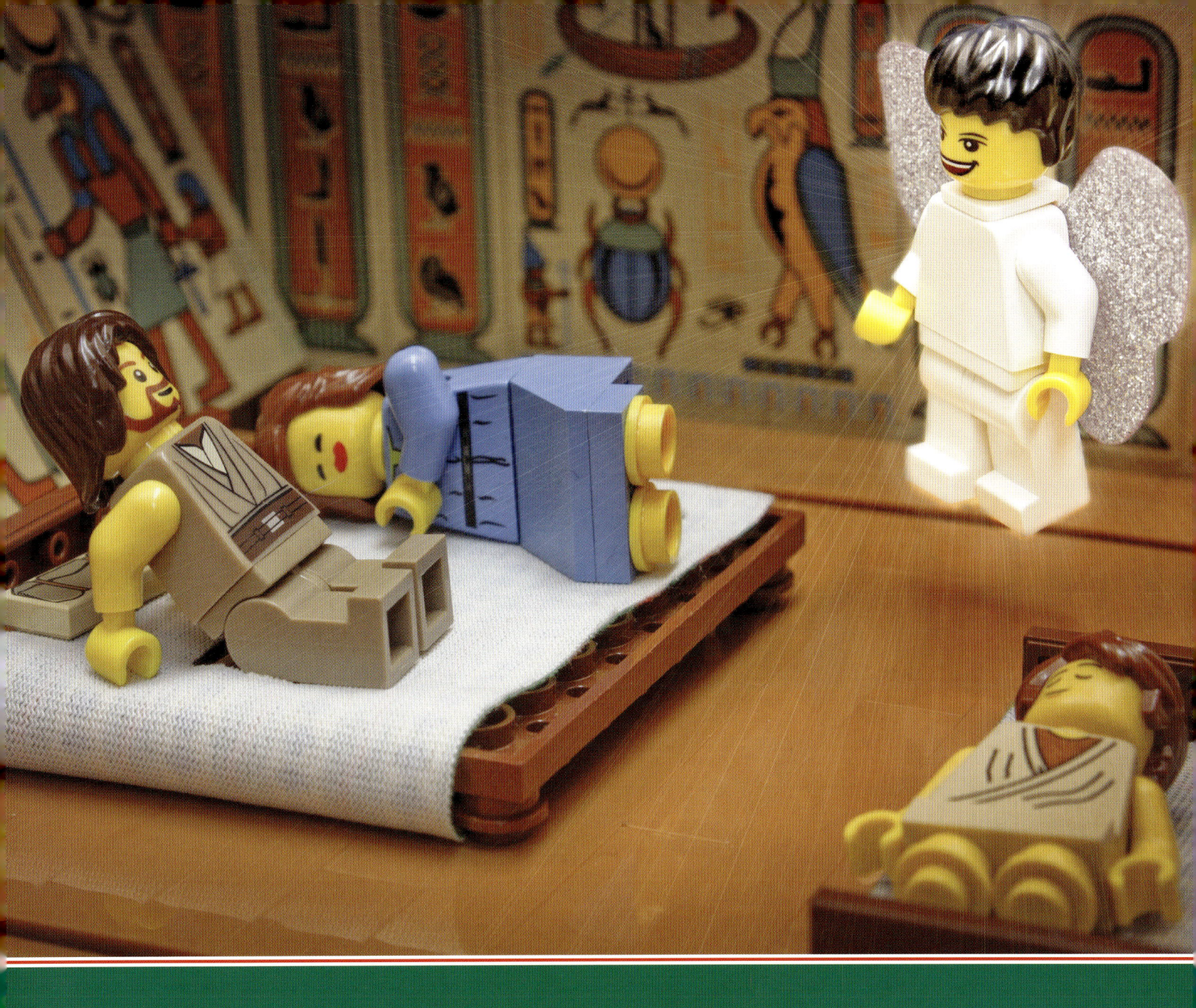

Later, when King Herod had died, an angel appeared to Joseph in Egypt and said, "Take the child and his mother back to the land of Israel, for those who wanted to kill the child are dead."

So Joseph took the child and his mother and set out from Egypt to return to Israel.

Joseph was warned in a dream not to go to Bethlehem, so they settled in Nazareth. There Jesus grew in strength and wisdom, and God's blessing was upon him.

Activity!

Can you find these ten brick pieces in the story? On which page does each appear? The answers are below.

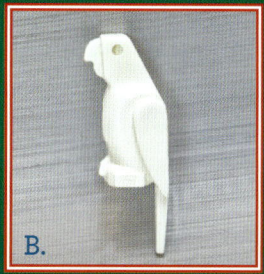

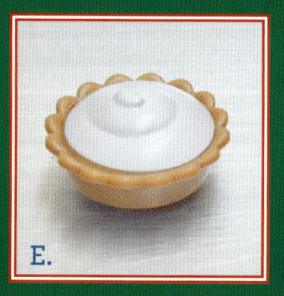

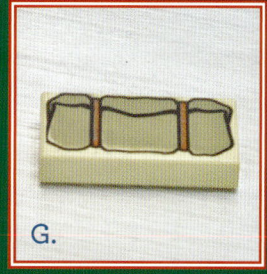

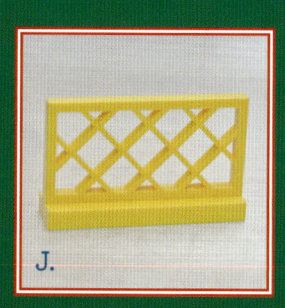

A.
B.
C.
D.
E.
F.
G.
H.
I.
J.

Answer key:

A: p.169, B: p.166, C: p.165, D: p.180, E: p.162, F: p.163, G: p.185, H: p.173, I: p.161, J: p.174

The End

Brendan Powell Smith is the author of the bestselling Brick Bible series for adults and six children's books in The Brick Bible for Kids series. His work has been hailed as "a spectacular twenty-first-century Biblical art masterpiece," by Rev. Wanda Lundy of the New York Theological Seminary. His work can be seen on his child-friendly website at www.brickbibleforkids.com.